LITTLE RABBIT'S
LOOSE TOOTH

LITTLE RABBIT'S LOOSE TOOTH

BY LUCY BATE
PICTURES BY DIANE DE GROAT

SCHOLASTIC INC.
New York Toronto London Auckland Sydney

ISBN: 0-590-11870-6

Text copyright © 1975 by Lucy Bate. Illustrations copyright © 1975 by Diane de Groat. This edition published by Scholastic Inc., by arrangement with Crown Publishers, Inc.

12 11   6/8

For Mike, Gabrielle, and Rebecca

Little Rabbit had a loose tooth. It was her first loose tooth, and it wiggled a lot. At suppertime Little Rabbit said, "You know I cannot eat carrots and beans. I have a loose tooth."

But Father Rabbit said, "Carrots and beans are very good for little rabbits."

"They are too hard," said Little Rabbit, "for little rabbits with a loose tooth."

"Oh?" said Mother Rabbit. "And what is soft enough for a little rabbit with a loose tooth?"

Little Rabbit thought for a while. There were strawberries in the refrigerator. "Strawberries," she said, "soft strawberries."

"You can have strawberries for dessert," said Mother Rabbit. "And you can chew the carrots and beans with your other teeth."

"Are you sure?" said Little Rabbit.

"I'm sure," said Mother Rabbit.

"Are you sure, Daddy?" asked Little Rabbit.

"I'm sure," said Father Rabbit. "I've done it myself."

TUESDAY

WEDNESDAY

On Wednesday she chewed watermelon with her loose tooth and lettuce with her other teeth.

On Thursday she chewed vanilla pudding with
her loose tooth
and cabbage with
her other teeth.

**THURSDAY
FRIDAY**

On Friday she chewed spinach with her other
teeth and chocolate ice cream with her loose
tooth, and the loose tooth
came right out in the chocolate ice cream.

"I have a tooth in my chocolate ice cream," said Little Rabbit.

"That's wonderful," said Mother Rabbit.

"It's about time," said Father Rabbit.

"What should I do with it?" asked Little Rabbit.

"You should take it out of your chocolate ice cream," answered Mother Rabbit.

Little Rabbit took the tooth out of the chocolate ice cream. "I have a window in my mouth," she said. "I can stick my tongue through it."

"That's amazing," said Mother Rabbit.

Little Rabbit put some chocolate ice cream in the window in her mouth.

"Look," she said. "I have a chocolate tooth in my mouth."

"How tasty!" said Father Rabbit.

Little Rabbit finished her dish of ice cream. Then she licked the chocolate ice cream off the tooth and took it to the sink and put the plug in the sink. She gave it a bath in cold water. Then she dried it with the dishtowel and took it back to the table.

"What should I do with my tooth?" she asked.

"Whatever you want," said Mother Rabbit.

"I could throw it away," said Little Rabbit.

"Or, you could put it under your pillow for the tooth fairy," said Mother Rabbit.

"Why should I do that?" asked Little Rabbit.

"When you are asleep the tooth fairy will take your tooth and leave you a present," said Mother Rabbit.

"Does the tooth fairy get to keep my tooth?"

"Yes, of course," said Mother Rabbit.

Little Rabbit put her tongue in the window in her mouth. Then she took her tongue out of the window. "What if I don't want the tooth fairy to keep my tooth?" she said.

"Then there's no point in putting your tooth under your pillow," said Mother Rabbit.

"I don't believe
in the tooth fairy, anyway,"
said Little Rabbit.

"No?" said Mother Rabbit.

"No," said Little Rabbit. "There are lots of things you can do with a tooth besides give it to a tooth fairy."

Little Rabbit took her tooth and went into her room and thought about the things she could do.

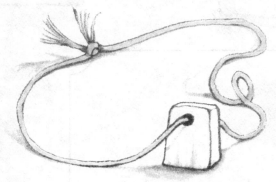

She could make a hole in it and put a string through it and wear it for a necklace.

But then she thought the tooth might break when she tried to make the hole.

She could paste it on a piece of paper and draw stars around it and hang it on her bedroom wall.

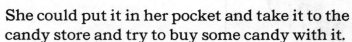

But then she thought that might look silly.

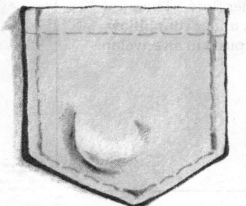

She could put it in her pocket and take it to the candy store and try to buy some candy with it.

But then she thought maybe the rabbit who owned the candy store would say that a tooth is not a penny.

Then Little Rabbit thought she could throw the tooth away, but she did not really want to do that, either.

Little Rabbit went into the living room where Mother Rabbit was playing the flute. "Mommy," she said, "what if I believe in the tooth fairy?"

Mother Rabbit put down her flute. "Then you'd better put your tooth under your pillow before you lose it. You can put it in an envelope if you want."

Little Rabbit found an envelope . . .

and put the tooth in it.

Then she went into her room . . .

and put the envelope under
her pillow.

Little Rabbit came back to the living room. "What kind of presents do tooth fairies leave?" she asked.

"Well," said Mother Rabbit, "what do you think?"

"I think they leave whatever they want," said Little Rabbit. "Money?"

"Not a lot of money," said Mother Rabbit.

Little Rabbit thought for a minute. "A penny?"

"Well, maybe a dime."

"A dime is smaller than a penny," Little Rabbit said.

"It's smaller but it's worth more," said Mother Rabbit. "A dime is worth ten pennies."

"I know that," Little Rabbit said. "I just wanted to make sure."

"Daddy," said Little Rabbit, "I believe in the tooth fairy."

Father Rabbit put down his newspaper so Little Rabbit could climb up into his lap. "And what do you think the tooth fairy wants with your tooth?"

"She wants to give me money," said Little Rabbit.

"Oh, I see," said Father Rabbit. "And what will she do with your tooth after she gives you money?"

"I think she will save my tooth and give it to a baby rabbit that was just born, and that's how little baby rabbits get teeth. Do you think that, Daddy?"

"Ah—" said Father Rabbit.

"Or," said Little Rabbit, "I think she will put my tooth up in the sky because it is such a shiny tooth, and that's how stars get made. Do you think that, Daddy?"

"We-l-l," said Father Rabbit.

"Really," said Little Rabbit, "I think she says a magic spell and she turns the tooth into a penny, I mean a dime. Do you think that, Daddy?"

"I think," said Father Rabbit, "that it is your bedtime."

"Okay, but would you please remind Mommy about my believing in the tooth fairy in case she forgets."

"I could," said Father Rabbit.

"My tooth is in an envelope under my pillow."

"That's good," said Father Rabbit.

"I have a window in my mouth."

"Window or no window," said Father Rabbit, "it is time for bed." He gave her a good-night kiss. "Good night, Little Rabbit."

"Good night, Daddy."